*To all men and women standing for freedom today,
so that all children may sleep safely tonight.*

"Tell me again, Momma! Tell me again!
About the angel, you know, the one God will send."
The Momma smiled and held her last little one tight
because they just had each other, at least for one more night.

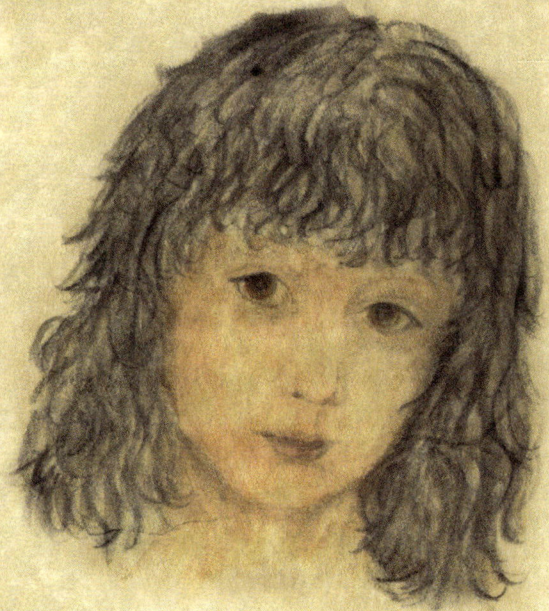

She thought of her family as she fought back the tears,
together no more and with many new fears.
In a country, with chains, led by an evil man,
she took a deep breath and with a smile began.
"The thunderous bombs and bright flashes is how God paved the way
for His Angels to come here and save us one day.
Angels armed with strength and all dressed in white
waiting for the time, when the moment is right.
For God sees everything and He hears people cry.
He sees what bad people do when they kill, hurt, and lie."

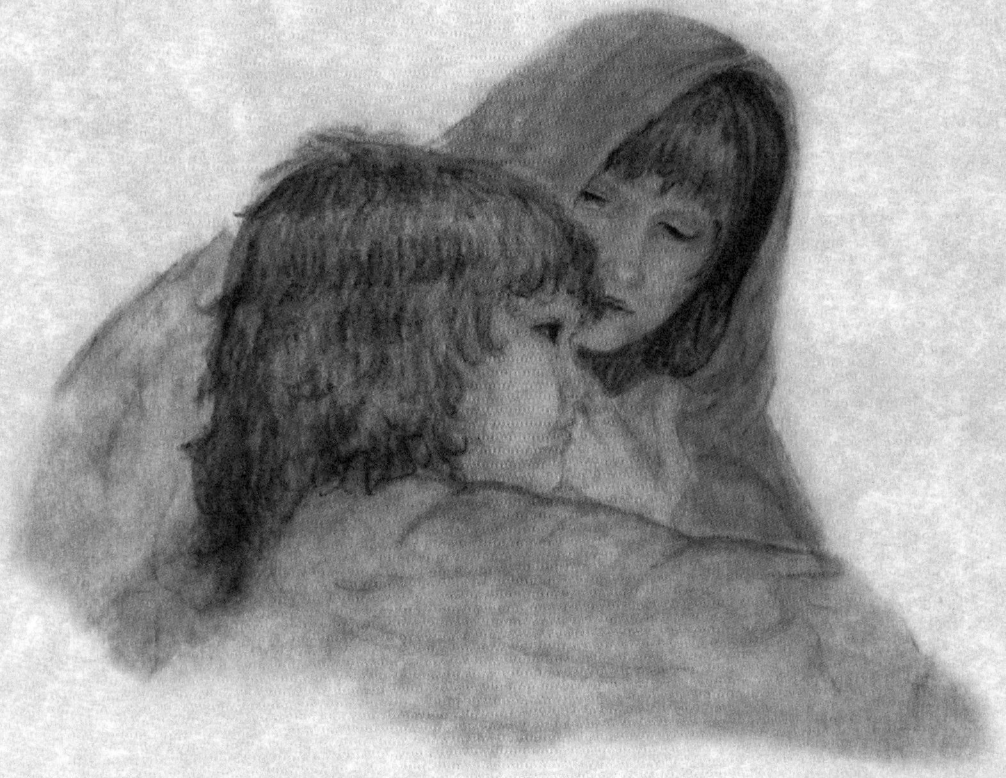

She looked up with the biggest brown eyes you've ever seen,
"I'm gonna pray that those angels get rid of all that are mean.
Answer our prayers, God, with someone from above,
send us some hope... some mercy... some love.
I won't stop praying for our angel of white,
for our big, strong protector may just come tonight!"

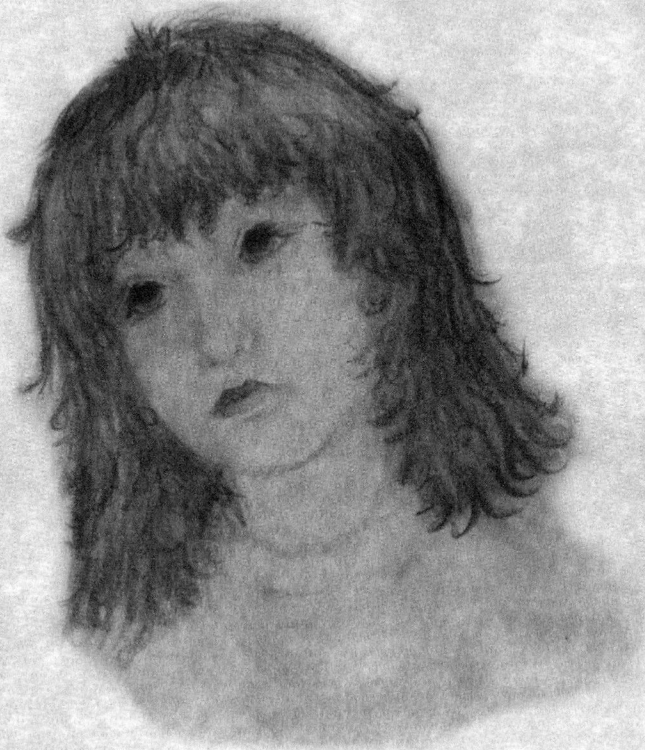

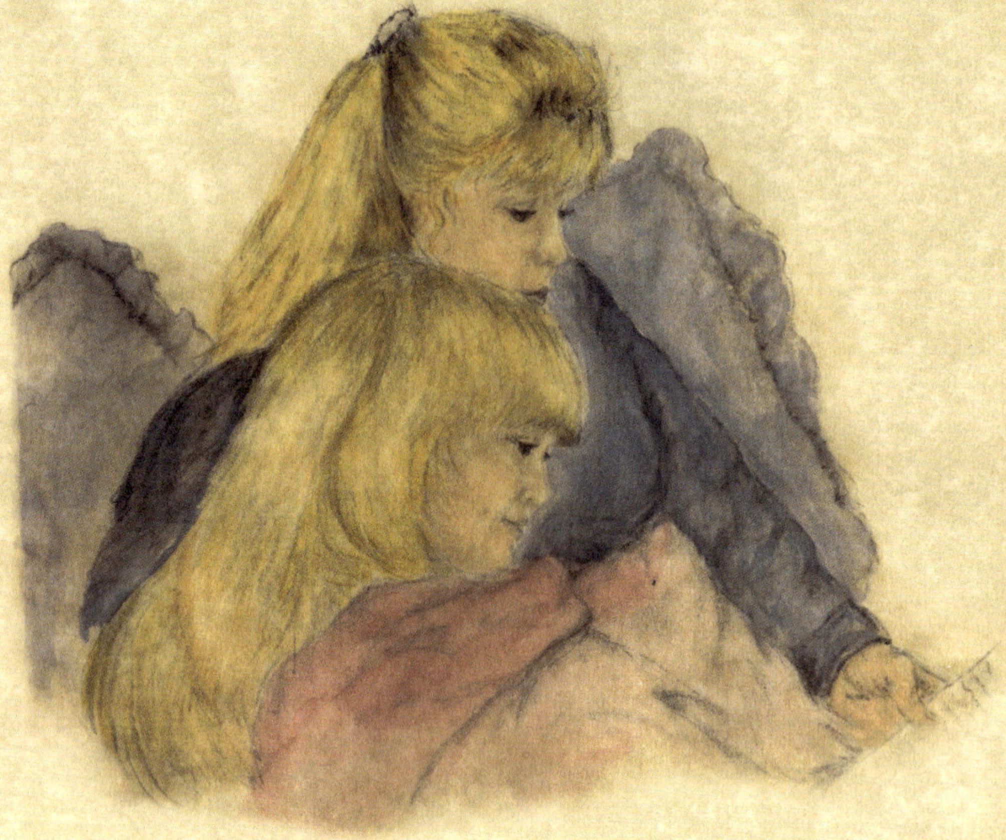

Half way 'round the world came another girls cry,
as she thought of her Daddy and when they said 'good-bye.'
"Tell me again, Momma! Tell me again!
About my Daddy, what words did he send?"

As they sat there together, their heads high and proud,
the Momma took a deep breath and read his letter out loud.
"I miss my best girls, I know you miss me, too,
but I'm here because I have an important job to do.
Hungry and scared are those that I seek,
all that are helpless, burdened, and weak.
I want to help others and let God use me
to liberate those people who don't live free.
In a land where people are hurt everyday,
I want to do my best to keep evil away."

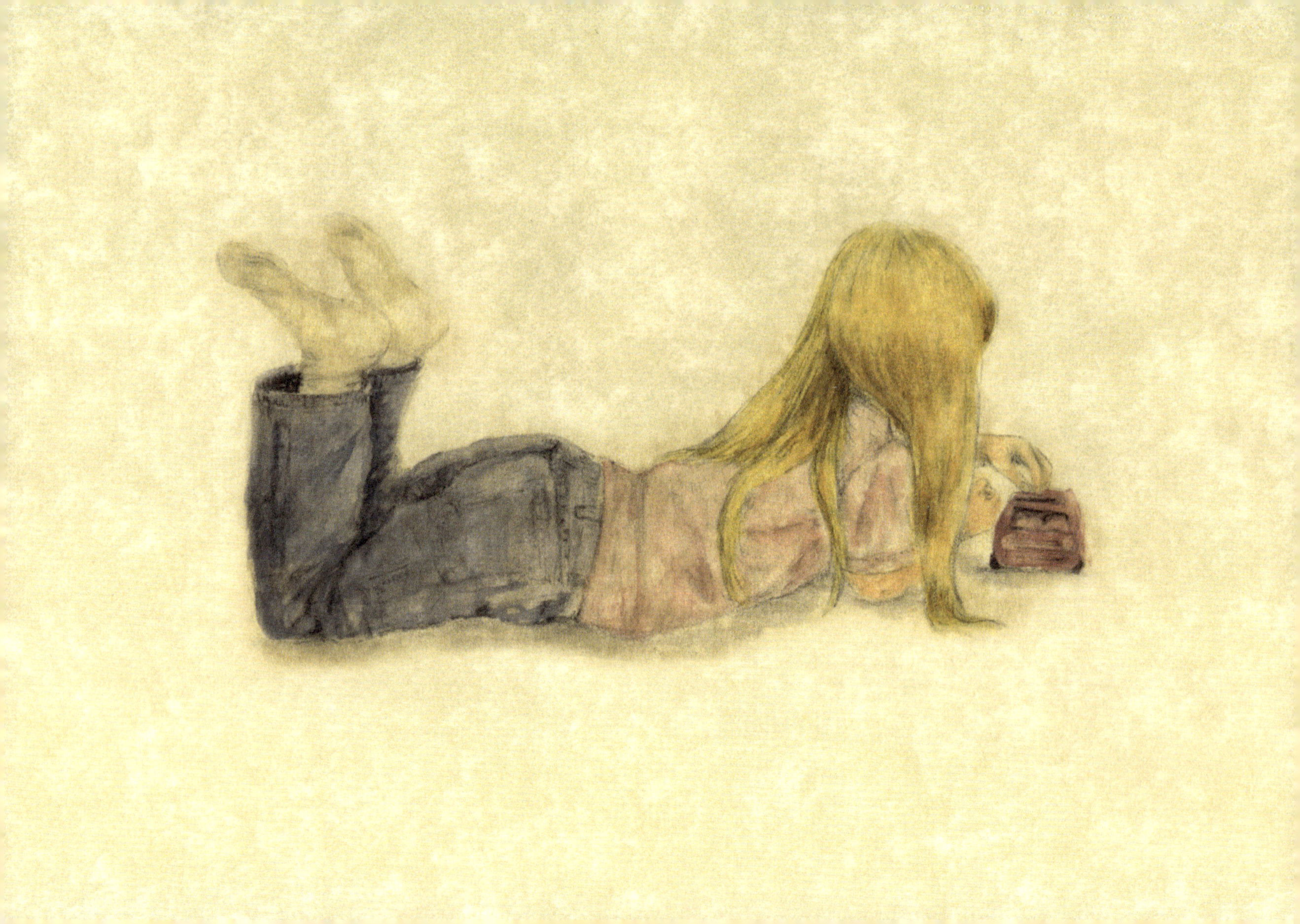

She looked up with the biggest brown eyes you've ever seen,
"I'm gonna pray God helps Daddy take care of all that are mean.
Answer our prayers, God, with someone from above,
help Daddy to give others hope... mercy... and love."
Securely and unselfishly as she played on the floor,
she said, "I'll share my Daddy, I guess they need Him more."

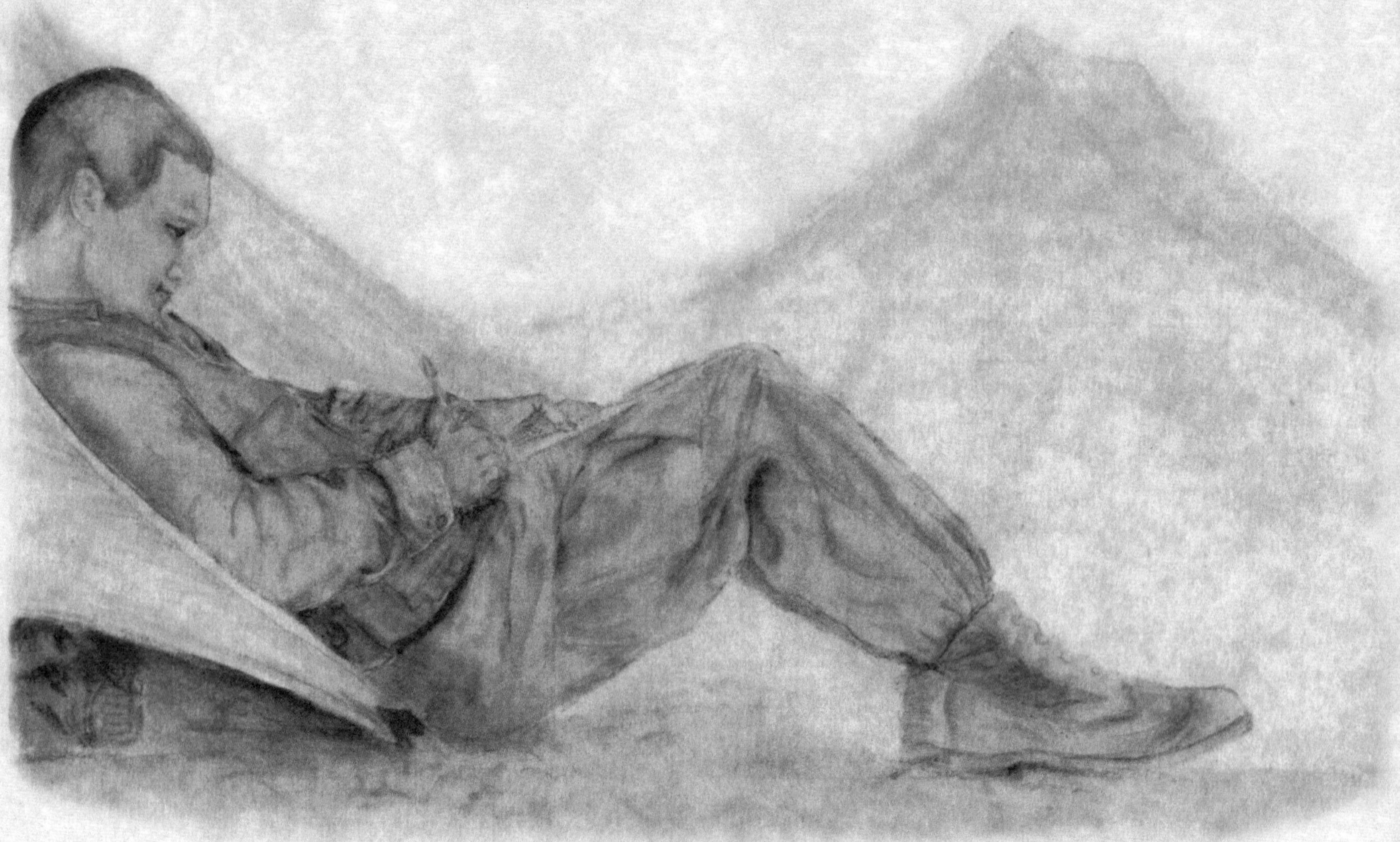

A humble tent is what the young man now called home
and he studied her picture whenever he was alone.
He kept telling himself, he had to do his part,
but thinking of them was breaking his heart.

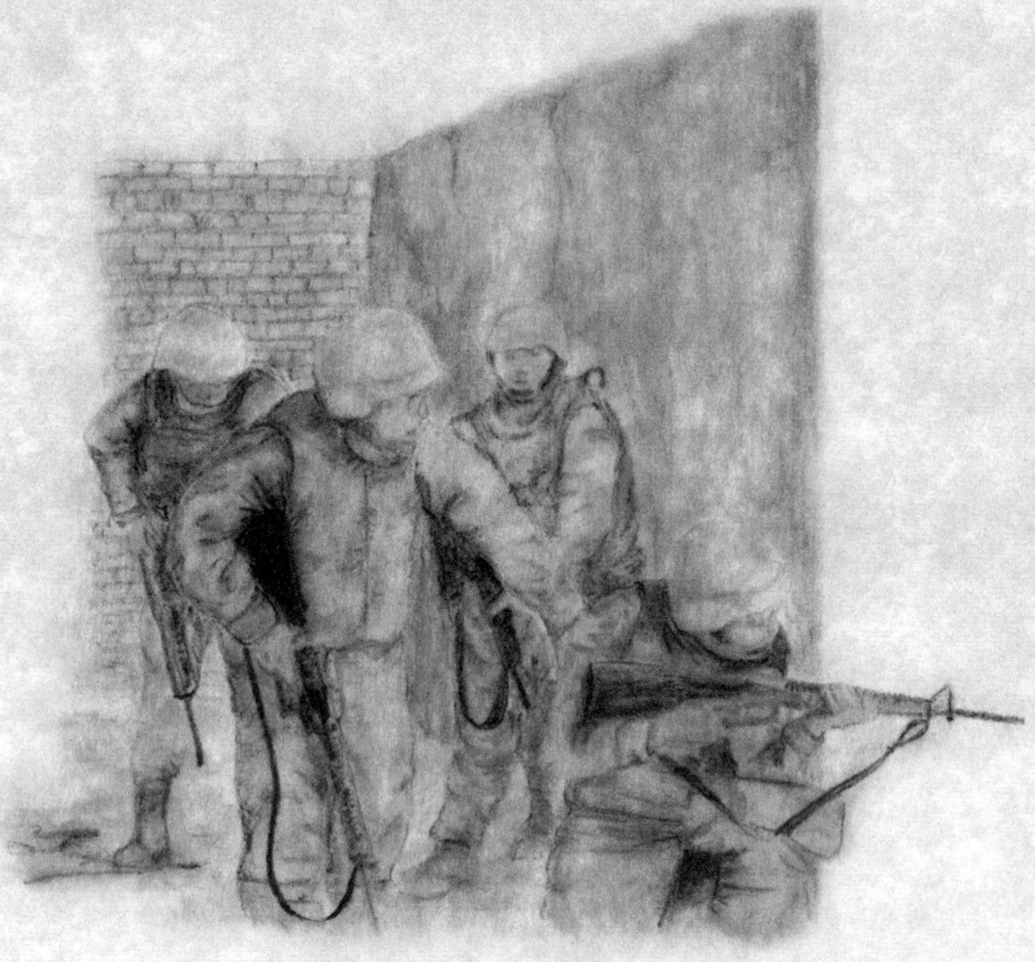

The young man grabbed his weapon and called into the night,
"Hurry up! Let's go! We'll be working till light."
Securing buildings and homes until the next day,
he thought of his girls a long ways away.
"What I would give, for a moment, to be out of this sand
and see those big brown eyes as she squeezes my hand."

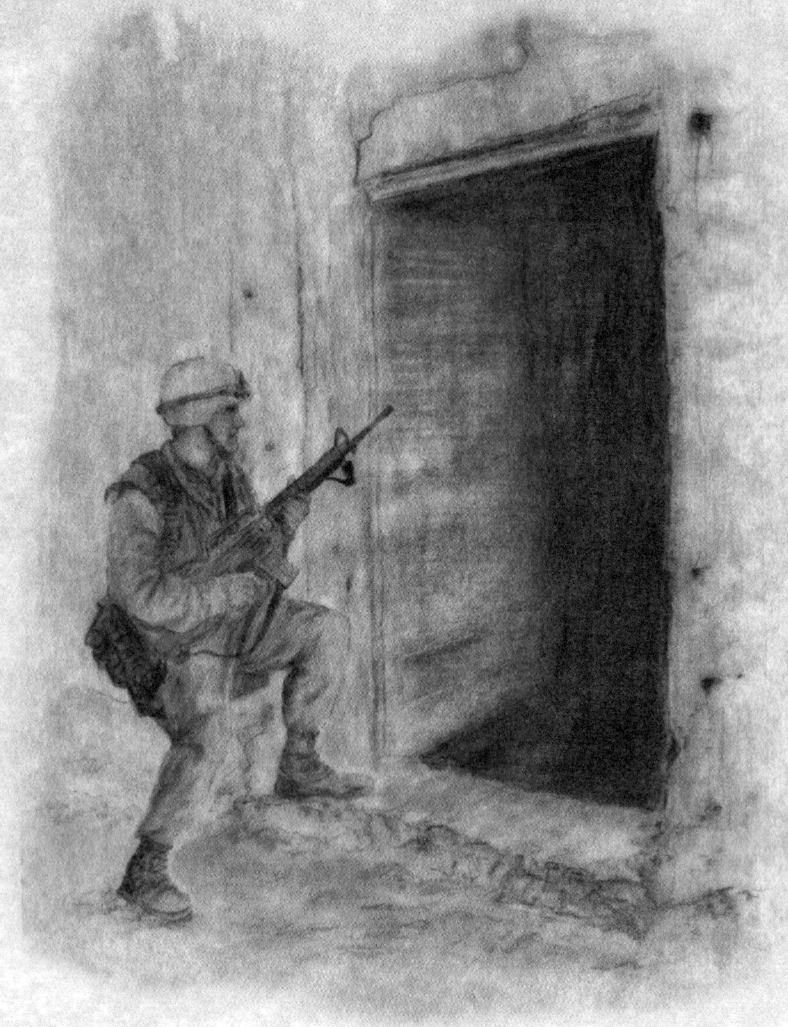

They came to the next house and carefully went thru the door,
to see a mother... a little girl... and nothing more.

At first their astonishment seemed to last for a while,
but finally Momma breathed deep and then gave him a smile.
The young man looked down and to his surprise,
he stared into the most beautiful big, brown eyes.

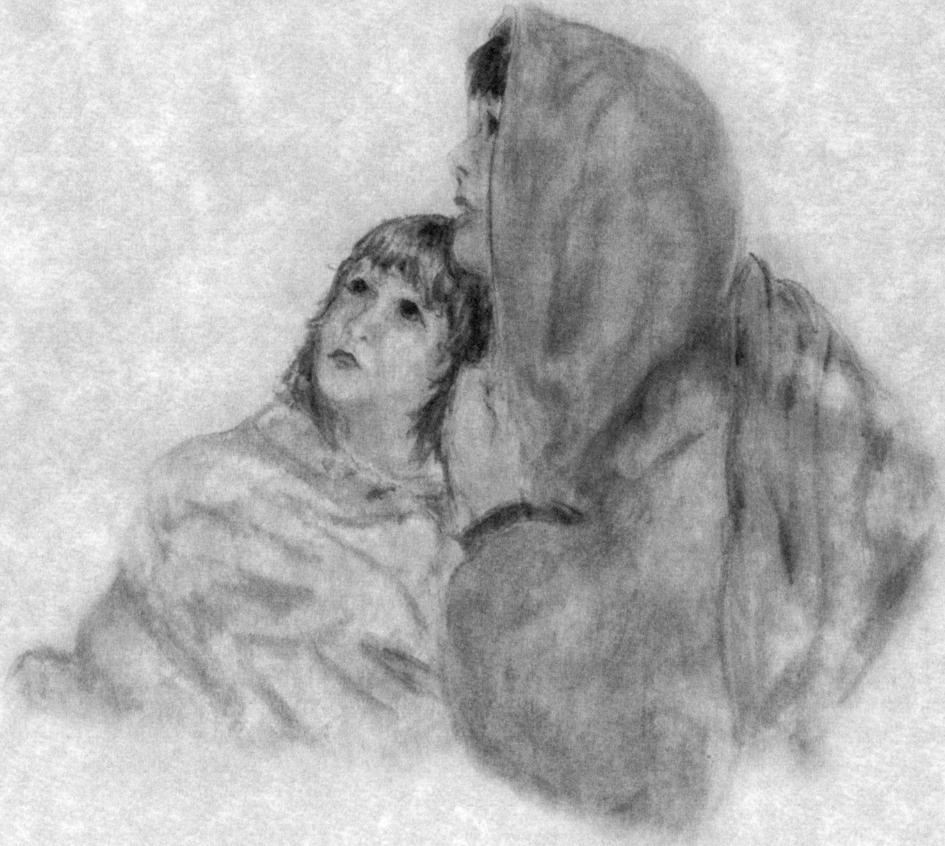

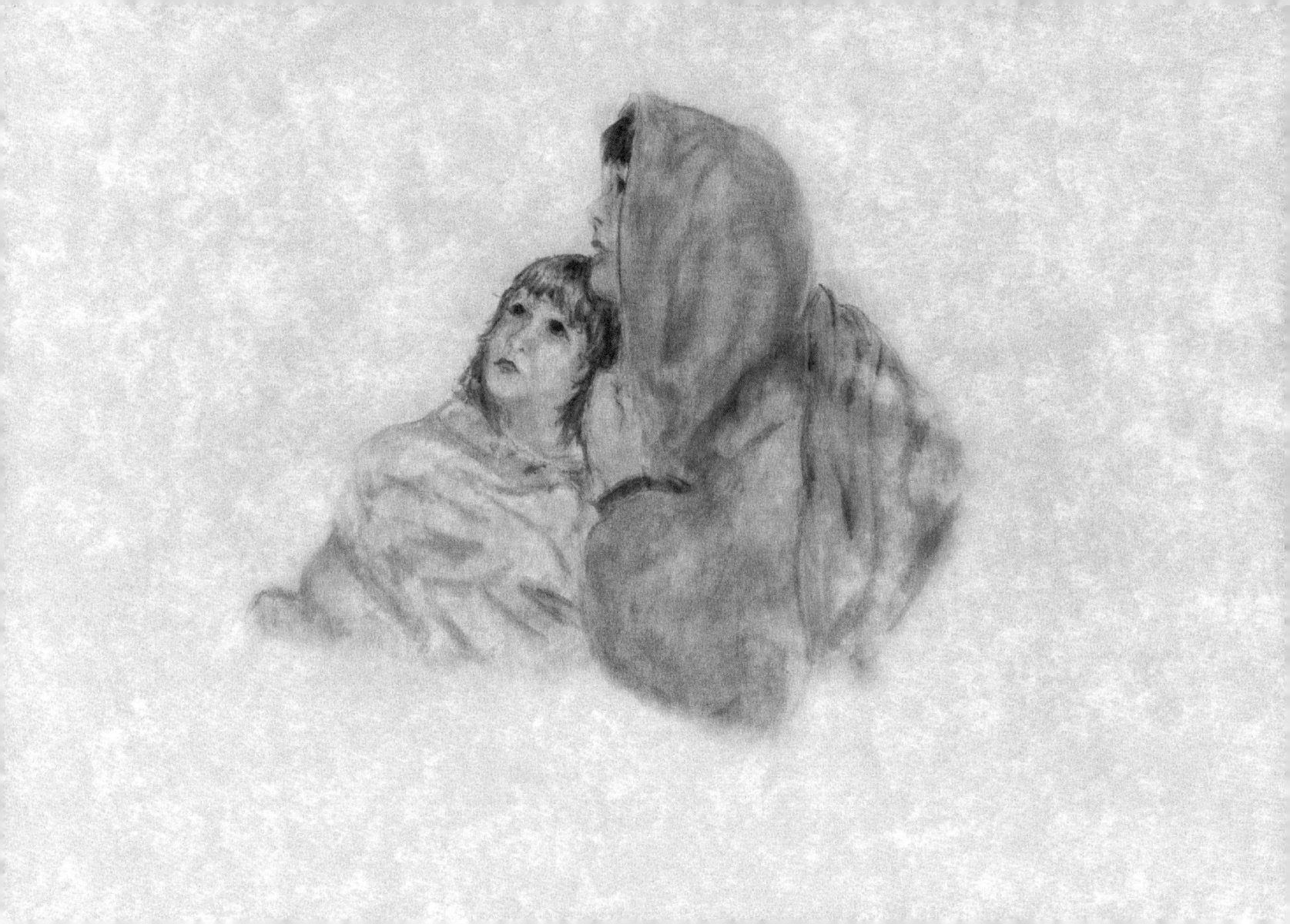

The little one grabbed his hand and squeezed as tight as she could.
They spoke two different languages, but they both understood.
The Momma nodded a thank you for saving their town,
and the little one said, "Momma, not all angels wear white...
this one wears brown!"